Shades of Ink

Flairs and Glairs

Publication House

"Shades of Ink"

ISBN No: " 978-93-90416-88-2"

1st Edition

Language – English and Hindi

Flairs and Glairs

Publication House

Regd. Under MSME Act.

Disclaimer

This is a work of fiction and solely represent the thoughts of the corresponding authors of the articles. Our editors have tried their best to edit the content of all the authors and chcck the plagiarism.

All the write-ups in this book are unique and are only published in this book.

In case any plagiarism or error is found, only the author is responsible alone, and not the publisher or the Compilers.

Cover Designing and Book Formatting

Shubham Shah and Ishani Agarwal

Co-Authors

Shubham Shah (Founder Flairs and Glairs)
Ishani Agarwal (Co-Founder Flairs and Glairs)

1. Subhalaxmi Senapati (Compiler)
2. Jackson Chang
3. Aishwarya Kulkarni
4. Divya Mishra
5. Sanya Tikarya
6. Sunita Singh
7. Sakshi Jain
8. Aditi Vyas
9. Ms Divya Dilip Shetty
10. Md Eftekar Ahmmed
11. Jay D (Jeetender Singh Ramgharia)
12. Ritu Jain
13. Sunidhi Shrivastava
14. Aman Raj
15. Pritha Konar
16. Muskaan Rafique
17. Megha Agarwal
18. Abhilash Giri
19. Dr. Srinidhi Govindarajan
20. Samriddhi Singh
21. Reshma Kausar Mohideen
22. Dr. Sarita Garg
23. Jashu Sankhlecha
24. Samruddhi Sharma
25. Adibah Masood
26. Srishti Srivastava
27. Jennifer Rebecca Paul
28. Darshitha P Mandoth

29. Aahan Agarwal
30. Janani
31. Dhanya Ravi
32. Akanksha Gupta
33. Ishaa Suresh
34. Swati Nayak
35. Diksha Motwani
36. Ganesh Sadashiv Patil
37. Kareena Verma
38. Bhuvan
39. Krishna Motwani
40. Adira Singh
41. Reema
42. Meharun Halidha. M
43. Jayashree Sahoo
44. Shivani M.R.Joshi
45. S. Vasha Varthini
46. Abhishek Ghosh
47. Seemabharti
48. Srijanie
49. Sujish Kandampully
50. Karan Singh
51. Kaushiki Sarkar

Shubham Shah

(Founder- Flairs and Glairs)

Shubham Shah, an entrepreneur at "Flairs & Glairs" a brand with dynamics in events organizing and cultural educational pan INDIA, is a 26yrs old guy who recently has entered the digital platform of imprinting emotions. He has initiated with

his own open mic platform to help budding poets and aspiring writers under his brand named as "Teekhe Zasbaaat"
He is a commerce graduate from the Bhagalpur City of Bihar.
He states Writing has impersonated him since childhood and he has now been writing for over a decade!
Cooking, on the other hand, is his passion! He also mentions, trying out new things just tickles him!
When asked sir, Why SPICY EMOTIONS?
He smiled and added, "agar jasbaat teekhe na ho toh wo jasbaat kahan" Spices are all that blends! So do his words!
As a chef, he presents to you his dish! Hot and freshly served! Taste it! Feel it! Enjoy it! You can also find his writing in the Book "Teekhe Zasbaaat" and 50+ Co-authored anthologies. With his passion to explore opportunities across Platforms, he is working with keen devotion and We wish him all the very best for his future ventures.
He is Featured in the **International Magazine De-Mode** for his upcoming solo novel.
He is **Approved by Ne8x for its Lit Fest,** and is a **Golden Star Awards 2020 Winner.**
He is an **India Book of Records Holder** for his Anthology **Satrang,** and has the **Grandmaster** title by **Asia Book of Records**, for the same.
He has also been featured in **Prabhat Khabar**, **Dainik Jagran** and other renowned Newspaper for his achievements.
He has also been awarded with **India Star Republic Award 2021.**
He has been a proud co-author to
India Book of Records (Title- Black)
World Book of Records (Title -15 Wonders of Poetries)
India Book of Records (Title - Aaina)

Vajra World Records Holder (Title - Gustakhi Maaf Hai)
High Range of Records Holder (Title - Gustakhi Maaf Hai)

Share your reviews on his

INSTAGRAM
@spicy_emotions
@shubham4shah

Or via email on
shubham2shah@gmail.com

To stay tuned to his work and opportunities follow his business Handles

INSTAGRAM FACEBOOK YOUTUBE

@flairsandglairs
@teekhezasbaaat

WEBSITE:
https://flairsandglairs.in/
https://flairsandglairs.com/

Ishani Agarwal

(Co-Founder- Flairs and Glairs)

Ishani Agarwal hails from the City of Joy, Kolkata.
She is the co-founder of her Community "Teekhe Zasbaaat" and Flairs and Glairs Publication.
Been a Compiler for 45+ Anthologies, she is in the process for more. Co-authored in 150+ Anthologies. She is a India Book of Records Holder, a Vajra World Records Holder, a High Range of Records Holder and a Bravo Record holder.

Approved by Ne8x for its Lit Fest 2020, and Literary Icon 2020. Also a Golden Star Awards Winner 2020.
She has also been awarded with India Star Republic Award 2021.
She has been featured by the National Magazine "Taree Zameen Par" with the title 'unstoppable'.
Also featured in the International Magazine DeMode for her upcoming solo novel, she is proud to write on social issues, and is happy with the love she is receiving.
Connect with her on Instagram: @Ishani_agarwal_quotes / @compilations_so_far

Subhalaxmi Senapati

Compiler

An understudy from Bhubaneswar presently seeking after her confirmation in Engineering. Her side interests are voyaging and understanding books. She went over composition to give herself a way musings to scatter. She loves composing since she appreciates wizardry in her life, not a wondrous fantasy, but rather a sorcery that would float her away from the cruel real factors of life. She puts stock in the statement "you got to express in your life".

Instagram-subhalaxmi_19

Bewildered Wonders

They are the most beautiful wonders
of the world,
I thank god for being lucky
but everyday looking at the intricacies
All i could say is a 'sorry'
For i am engulfed by thorns of envy
So are the wonders, in the sombre abyss.
Just a crumbled touch of the fierce
And the fabulous wonder, fears
For its felicity, tumbles off.
The woes and weeping,
Chimes in their shredded hearts,
Shrouded by stones and marbles.
The wonders just wish for lovely hues
To be painted on their bare canvasses.
They long to be graciously garnished,
In the sublime shades of the Almighty
They yearn to be cyanided with peace,
And not with toxic chemicals in air.
All they want is a caress,
On the parched walls and stones
To bless the blemishes and burns
For they wish to rise amidst the wreck,
And unshackle the muffled reality
That obliterated their beauty.

Colours

Drawn with shades of colour
Red, magenta, white
A ray of pitch black too.

I chose red to embellish the walls of your heart.
To tell you that red doesn't symbolize blood and war
But stands for deep affection and love.

I made sure that colour doesn't spill out when my quivering hands touched the edges with magenta.
To tell you that love isn't only about promises or commitment, but is about compassion and harmony, spreading kindness and strengthening intuition.

I chose white to tell you that love is about all the sacrifices we made for each other.
How we imbibed tranquillity and escaped from the chaos.

I made final touch up with black.
Yes, black, to tell you that when u will be engulfed by darkness, i will be there for u to lean on
To remind you, how we conquered the wrath of demons and lived happily ever after.
Drawn with shades of colour
Embellished your heart
With my colours of love.

Jackson Chang

Jackson Chang is an MA student enrolled in the English Program at the National Central University in Taiwan. He is interested in children's literature, poetry and translation.

Jackson has been writing poetry since 2018 and admires the work of Rabindranath Tagore, famous for his poems and songs, and for being the first Asian to win the Noble Prize in 1913. Furthermore, he admires the work of Hafez Shirazi and Pablo Neruda, known for their ghazals and sonnets."

Phoenix

Born in the fire and flame,
Flying to the sky with its splendid wings.

When seeing it fly in the sky,
People consider it immortal and holiness.

Born as a king or a queen in Nature,
How beautiful God creates you.

Pride and confidence are your weapon,
With the flame on your body.

Fly! Fly!
Fly toward the eternal, paradise, and heaven.

Divya Mishra

She is a kind of person who believes in transforming every emotion into poetry, with a passion for helping people heal and get motivated through her words.

I have always loved you

From the day I chose you
To the day I felt you
To the day I met you
I have always loved you

From that late night, voice calls with you
To those updated video calls to you
To those "turn around!" calls for you
I have always loved you

From getting hurt by you
To not being consoled by you
To still not regretting over choosing you
I have always loved you

From those mutual future plans with you
To your losing interest over a few
To crying over that uncertain future with you
I have always loved you.

Sanya Tikarya

She is a doctor learning homeopathic medicine. Apart from her studies she has a passion for writing and put her heart in it. She has a personality of fresh air, innocence and pure simplicity. She owns the website www.sanyaTikarya.in where, she publishes her writings. Not a master she likes to call herself, but has a clear command over words. Her poems indulge readers in a manner that it brightens up their day. She always tries to incarnate her feelings into words, to reach the heart and soul of every person reading it.

अजनबी तुम बहुत अपने से

अरे ओ! अजनबी तुम बहुत अपने से लगने लगते हों
बिना जान पहेचान ,जब तुम मेरी फिकर सी करने लगते हों
तुम बहुत आपने से लगने लगते हों
जब दर्द मेरा तुम प्यार से बाटा सा करते
बिना खामयाजा दिए मेरी गलतियों पर पर्दा से करते हों
तुम बहुत अपने से लगने लगते हों
बिना किसी दुनियादारी से जब तुम मेरे गिले शिकबे सुना करते हों
हाँ तुम बहुत अपने से लगने लगते हों
वो कुछ पलों की मुलाकात में तुम अजनबी से मेरे हमदर्द से बनजाते हों
हाँ तुम बहुत अपने से लगते हो
हाँ इस वीरान नगरी में तुम बहुत आपने से लगते हों !!

वो भी क्या दिन थे

ख्वाब थे अपने , रंग थे सच्चे ,
बचपन से ही हम बड़े थे अच्छे;
रोज़ नए नए से वादे ,
नए रंग में घुले इरादे ।
प्यारी दुनिया ,सच्चे वादे ,
हम रानी , हम थे शहज़ादे ।

बारिश की वो पहली बूंदे
भीगे अखियों को हम मूंदें
होठों से छूती वह बारिश ,
उफ्फ पगली सी नन्ही ख्वाइश ।।

काठ के गुडिया , नन्हे चिड़िया
पहली दीवाली की वो फूलझड़ियाँ
घोड़े गधे सब लगे समान ,
जहाँ भी डर हो जय हनुमान ।

मोम के रंगों की रंगोली
कागज़ की नाव , पहली वो होली

अभी मुझमें सब बस्ते हैं ,
लिखते लिखते हम हस्ते हैं ।।"

Sunita Singh

A Published Writer
Simple, easy going & friendly. Playing with words please don't relate them to my personal life.
Writing is my passion.
Writer on Pratilipi app.
Master in Hindi from Himachal University."

हद में

गर सब रह ले हद में
तो बात ही कुछ और होगी
न करो सब मनमानी
न खेलो प्रकृति से
न कटो पेडो को
न जलाओ प्रकृति को
हद में रहकर तो देखो
अमन ही अमन है।"

शायरों की दुनिया

बड़ी ही अजीब होती है
जुबां ख़ामोश रहती है
कलम शोर करती है
शायर खुद में ही गुम
खुद में ही गमगीन रहते है
उनकी एक अलग दुनिया
अलग अंदाज होते हैं।
बेफिकर, बेपरवाह, बेसबब
से दिखते हैं पर हर दिल
का दर्द बखूबी जानते ह

Aditi Vyas

Aditi Vyas is a passionate Writer who along with Writing loves Painting, Singing and Reading.
She is an ambitious girl and is trying her best to become someone who can help others by her Works.
She is on Quora as Aditi vyas and on Instagram as aditivyasav"

(1)

12th June it was and there was light on all the sides,
We were in Joy as wedding was there last night..

13th June when we came back to our ordinary life,
But still there was a light as were buying a flat in the city sight.

We were Dreaming and Daddy was working,
He went Surat all alone for the last time

14th June it was, the BLACK DAY of my life,
I got a call from someone close to my life

He told me in the morning that he was all FINE,
But he never knew, how we reached there on time.

He was on bed all in sleep,
And tears were coming from my sleepy eyes.

All I wanted was his warm hug,
That I got on my worst FATHER'S DAY

I wished him and his THANK YOU BETU made me cry,
I couldn't stay there even for a while...

100's of people were there to wipe my cries but all I wanted was a single person to make me smile

I remember how we folded him in a bed sheet to take him in Car,
And, it was the day when I said my DREAM PLACE a final goodbye...

It was Difficult but not more than his life.
After all I love him more than my life... More than my life

Ms Divya Dilip Shetty

Divya is a soulful writer with fine words. Her poems are all about Nature, Inspiration, Fiction & Love too. By way of her words she tries to touch the hearts of her adorable readers.

Why Is She So Beautiful?

The exquisite nature brings solace
To the dispirited souls,
The void, it fills with its tenderness
Making everyone to rejoice,
The dense green foliage around
Has deepest tales hidden,
The enduring aroma of it
Spreads zeal in the air,
The mountain peak touches the heavens
Giving contentment to the globe,
The cascades cools the weather
Quenching the thirst of its creatures,
The creatures ramble & prowl
In the womb of the forest,
The blossoming flowers twirl
Making the birds croon,
Feels like the nature is a godsend
& to treasure it for lifetime.

In The Dusk

The dusk brought the happiness
One's heart craves for,
Together amidst the busy life
There came a light of joy,
Sparkling on the streets
As well as on the frown faces,
The tired body waits for relaxation
The breeze gives a sudden warm hug,
The time that seemed to be running slowly
Runs fast now,
Patience comes to an end
& destiny seems to be so close,
The heart waited so long
To see the charm on the faces of loved ones,
To reach home as soon as possible
& to converse with them,
In the dawn the hearts that had left home
The dusk reunites all of them.

Md Eftekar Ahmmed

Md Eftekar Ahmmed is working as a scholer at HNB Garhwal University. He won national award MANF for his research work. He is University chess player also along with writer. He completed his M.A with distinction.

Tortured

When I was five, my Mom sent me
At torture centre along with bag and baggage.
Since little by little I started losing my Mom's care and love,
I was taught how to behave just like adult at five.

Very first day I met with Western language
Since that day I started losing my swadesi tongue.
I was handed over a tuft of treatises,
Even my fat bag helpless to digest such huge treatises.

I was forced to seat in classroom,
Guarded by massi (maid) like a prisoner.
I was forced not to talk, not to move,
First time I lost my freedom over toilets.

My Mom paid them handsome fees for torture,
Because Mom loved me much more.
My Mom getting poorer and poorer
And my Torturers getting richer and richer.

They were not stopped here only,
They took test also how well I am tortured.
If I fail to satisfy their torture level,
They sent threats letters to my Mom.

Every day I was lined up thrice for foods,
Just one dry bread and palm rice they threw.
I was only a silent observer in that cage
Where every parts of my body were chained.

On my releasing day at sixteen,
I was handed a piece of paper.
That piece of paper was my releasing certificate,
Still that paper is decorated on my walls.

Jay D (Jeetender Singh RamGharia)

Co-author Jay D (Jeetender Singh RamGharia) is a good writer from Rajasthan. He has been writing poetry/songs/quotes for a longtime as his passion.
Follow on InstaGram:- @jd_writer13. Subscribe YouTube Channel:- Jay D13 Music"

ज़िंदगी

बस अब दिल की तसल्ली वास्ते ख़ुद के लिए ख़ुद से बोलूंगा
कभी किसी के आगे अपने दिल का भेत ना खोलूंगा
अक्सर बुरा लगता है मेरी बातों का लोगों को
एक बार फिर कलम- ऐ - जज्बातों को किताब में ही खोलूंगा

खुश रह आबाद रह
ना रंग–ऐ–ज़िन्दगी तबाह कह
मुस्कान को रख हर वक्त चेहरे पे
बस उदासियो को अलविदा कह

चेहरे पर मुस्कान लिए वक्त गुजर जाए
पर ऐ–ज़िन्दगी फिर भी खफा है मुझसे
शिकायत ना करना चाहता हूं
फिर भी कोई वास्ता ना है शायद मुझसे"

ख्वाहिशें

उमर का तकाजा ना रख–ऐ–बंदेया
मंजिल का ख्याल कर
वक्त रहते मिल जाए आसमान उड़ने को
अपनी ख्वाहिशों का ख्याल कर

उम्र के साथ बढ़ते है सिलसिले तजुर्बों के
वरना अक्सर कुछ सीखने की चाह में
ज़िन्दगी ही खत्म हो जाती है

हुआ तब तक इंतजार किया उसके आने का
हर लम्हा गुज़रा यूं के हम उसके बिना जीना भी सीख गए

कुछ अल्फ़ाज़ मेरे ऐसे जो
मेरे साथ कोई शुरू करे
मेरे अधूरे रहे शब्दो को
वो अपने अल्फाजों संग पूरा करे"

Ritu Jain

Ritu Jain is a student of Delhi University. She has always been amused with the power of words in conveying myriad thoughts. In the initial years of her writing phase, she insists upon continuous exploration of her diverse thoughts and is trying to give meaning to them.

(1)

"Diving deep into the ocean of questions were my whats and ifs,
Didn't reach them even after listening to their sniffs.

For once I moved towards the rising sun,
only to become brighter with no regret over the death of the drowning one."

(2)

"the world condemned yet she dared
their eyeballs mesmerizingly glared, when her success aired
not a day she was lazy, because she really cared"

Sunidhi Shrivastava

An eighteen year old girl, with lots of dreams and aspirations. She writes to convey her feelings. She loves drawing. Apart from this, she is a trained Bharatanatyam dancer.

(1)

"My mommy's garden is her happy place,
It makes her feel very content and cherry, in so many different ways.

She waters them, as if they're her own children,
No doubt, looking at a beautiful blooming flower feels like heaven.

She loves them like they're a part of her and she handles them with care,
If you're ever having a thought of plucking a flower from her garden, don't you dare!

The flowers here, seems to be conversating with each other,
There's blooming a little bud; yay the pink rose now has a cute baby brother.

The leaves are smiling behind their greenery,
Ah, the view looks no less than mesmerizing scenery.

Oh here's the yellow one, such an alluring beauty,
How to consider any one of them as the best, they're all so pretty.

The misty smell of the wet soil, everyone fancy that,
Two lovely butterflies sitting on the rose petals for some casual chit-chat.

They're rich in colours; they're redolent and divine,
They don't ask for anything much, just some water, and some sunshine.

Look at those captivating floret, let them bloom and flourish,
They're so tender and soft, protect them and nourish.

My mommy's garden is her happy place,
It makes her feel very content and cherry, in so many different ways.

Aman Raj

Aman Raj was born in Jamshedpur Jharkhand and raised in Banka Bihar. He is a 2nd year medical student in Jaipur the pink city of Rajasthan. He loves to study his favourite subject Biology and some motivational books. In his free time he loves to draw, write all kind of write-up. He loves to hear music to relax his mind as it is a best way to gain lot of positive energy and he have a bit interest in gardening. He loves to spend my day with nature with lots of busy schedule.

My dream.

I want to become a doctor. Being one is not only my dream but also my parent's. I don't wish to be the wealthiest and most highly graduated doctor the world's ever seen but I want to be one who will serve her people and country in a true manner. In fact I don't want to be a doctor for only patients but for the needy too. Although I know it isn't everyone's cup of tea to be faithful, humane and achieve great degrees at the same time but it is worth a try. I always want to feel the pride of being loyal to my patients and my duty.

Well it's not always the same story from the beginning in fact it was totally different. When I was a little girl, I didn't actually wanted to be a doctor and never was worried about it. All I used to think was being a singer. Of course that was a dream for me which I wished to come true. It included of me always singing silly songs and even recording and playing them back. But soon circumstances changed, I grew up and came to know my real destiny. Although I showed interest in studies from the beginning but singing was something which I used to do every time, whether I be studying or playing. Many may call it as craziness but this was me as a kid. But as I mentioned earlier, I grew up to know where I belong and concentrated on it.

For now, for real I have a different dream and that is I want to become a doctor.

Pritha Konar

Pritha Konar, the writer has been a literature student, born in West Bengal and brought up in different states due to frequent postings of her father, writes usually in English with a few poems in Hindi too. She is also a Classical Dancer. Most of her poetries are in the form of blank verse and a few have been given a rhyming touch. Her works are also published in five books. Her writings also include short stories and quotes. She started writing during her graduation in English honours which gave her the base to enter the world of writing. Then she started weaving the words into poetries and stories.

The Happy Moment...

She was always apprised about the benefits of being a single girl child. Those three words were like burbs penetrating her heart. In reproach, decided not go home on Rakhi vacation. Next day she was informed by the hostel warden to visit Principal's office. Startled she, when her parents entered holding a boy's hand. Soon she found her exhilaration when she found she was no more a single girl child. He was none other than her biggest surprise of her life, her brother, her parents' adopted child."

The Last Page...

..Used to travel long distance, her college in different state, first year where she entered like a tomboy, life rained surprises when she met her senior at blood donation camp, with whom she experienced sitting behind a boy for the first time in activa, shared her silence and smile, sensed love. He became the reason for whom she dressed in a girly manner, in the final year she not only graduated in English but graduated in life cycle too as her proposal to him made her his fiancé. Her memory diary's last page.. "

Megha Agarwal

Megha, a girl from the city of Assam is fond of writing. She wrote many poems and currently is working on a short story cum poetry named "INTO THE PAST". She also wrote one such earlier named "SCHOOL LOVE" which got more than 2k views on the online platform Wattpad. More than holding a book, she loves to hold a pen.

You can follow her on Wattpad- MeghaAgawal953"

फिर भी यूहीं मुस्कुरा लिया करती है।

आँखों में नमी सी है,
फिर भी अक्सर हमें खुश रखा करती है,
चाहे मन ना हो,
फिर भी यूहीं मुस्कुरा लिया करती है।

बिन कहे ही सब समझ लेती है,
आख़िर प्यार जो इतना करती है।
हम ना भी समझ पाए उन्हें,
फिर भी मुस्कुरा लिया करती है।

कुछ खाने का मन है,
जब कहते है,
वह "कुछ" को भी ला देती है।
उनकी ज़रूरतों से पहले मांग पूरी होती है हमारी,
फिर भी अक्सर यूहीं मुस्कुरा लिया करती है।

कहती तो है,
दुनिया देखो,
कुछ बन कर दिखाओ,
हालांकि दूर भेजने से वह डरती है।
फिर भी हमारी ख़ुशी के लिए यूहीं मुस्कुरा लिया करती है।

डॉक्टर के पास ना जाने के सौ बहाने दे जाती है,
दर्द चाहे उन्हें ज़्यादा ही हो,
ठीक हूं कहकर,
अक्सर यूहीं मुस्कुरा लिया करती है।

घर लेट पहुंचे तो चिंता कर बैठती है,

आखों के सामने आने पर,
कैसा था दिन पूछ लिया करती है।
हंसकर पापा से झूठ केह जाती है,
वह मां ही है,
जो अक्सर यूहीं मुस्कुरा लिया करती है

Abhilash Giri

Abhilash is from Varanasi, Uttar Pradesh. He has completed his basic education and pursued B.Sc. in Interior Designing from there itself. He is a trained and aspiring actor. He started writing few months back and this is going so good so far.

भारतीय सैनिक

धन्य थे वो सैनिक जिन्होंने आज़ादी दिलाई,
कि थी उन्होंने ख़ून पसीने की लड़ाई ।

लेकर सीना खड़े हो जाते थे गोला बारूद के सामने,
देखकर उनको, दुश्मन लगता था थर थर कांपने ।

वीरता और बहादुरी का वो ग़ज़ब का मिसाल दे गए,
आने वाली पीढ़ी को हिम्मत देकर वो बड़ा कमाल कर गए ।

मरने से पहले एक एक ने सौ सौ को मारा,
याद रखेगा उन्हें हमेशा ये भारत देश हमारा ।

तिरंगा को झुकने न दिया कभी,
देश का हौसला टूटने न दिया कभी,
डटे रहे सरहद पे, जब तक अंतिम सांस थी,
यूंही नहीं कोई शहीद कहलाता, ज़रूर उनमें भी कोई बात थी ।

सीने में लग जाए कितनी भी गोली,
वो बोलते थे बस इन्क़लाब की बोली ।

देश के हर प्रांत से कोई न कोई लड़ने आता था,
पता रहता था उन्हें कि बचना अब मुश्किल है, फिर भी वो लाल फ़क्र से मुस्कुराता था ।

पता नहीं था घर वालों को कि लाल उनका वापस लौट कर आएगा,
बस फ़क्र इस बात का था कि अगर जान चली गई जंग में तो देश के लिए शहीद कहलाएगा ।

अगर हमारे देश पर वार करने की हिम्मत कभी भी आई,
याद रखना आज़ादी, 65, 71 और कारगिल की लड़ाई ।

जिस दिन तू सोचा आंख उठाने के लिए, उस दिन तू हारेगा,
ये नया हिन्दूस्तान है, घर में घुसकर मारेगा।

दूर रहना सरहद से, अगर पास आए तो ध्यान रखना अपनी जान का,
हर जगह सरहद पर घूम रहा है शेर हिंदूस्तान का ।"

शब्द कम पड़ जाए उनके बारे में लिखते हुए,
लिखना तो दूर, गर्व होता है देश को उनपे, बस उनके बारे में सोचते हुए ।

Dr. Srinidhi Govindarajan

Dr. Srinidhi Govindarajan is a passionate poet cum doctor who loves to read, write and create some splendid pieces of poetry drawing inspiration from her day to day life experiences. She is a doctor at Kasturba Medical College, Manipal University. She also expresses her creativity through drawings and by playing the Saraswati Veena. She hopes to portray her emotions and traditions in her art form.

About paati, dearest grandmother

Arthritis hit her hard,
Her joints screamed of pain,
Her cells cried for relief,
Depressed, discouraged and dejected.

She lay on the wooden bed,
Gazing at the ceiling fan,
Pondering over the beauty of life,
Her thoughts flew around the world and beyond,
Like a free pigeon in the summer sky,
Calm, still and serine.

Wrinkles masked her tender face,
Adored with a bright graceful smile,
Uttering always,
The name of god,
Ever grateful, never complaining.

Her pain couldn't be cured,
Her life couldn't be saved,
But her spirit will be preserved
And carried upon, for generations to come."

About thatha, granddad dearest

A picture means a thousand words,
What about a thousand years?
The wrinkles that mask a gentle smile,
The memories that live in pages of a distant past.
Remembering the untold tales of his heart.
Of love and loss,
Of passion and promises,
Of faith and trials,
Of falls and triumphs,
The million experiences the define human existence,
The million people that passed his way,
He smiles at it all,
Preserving all that he can in the abyss of his failing memory,
His weary bones brittle with bearing the weight of a thousand years,
His skin glowing with the first pale rays of the sun,
He breathes it all in,
Whispers a silent prayer of gratitude
For a long life, well lived. "

Muskaan rafique

She is a lawyer who had a keen interest in writing.
Her love for writing has also made her start an instagram page, she feels writing is a beautiful way of expressing yourself and keeping oneself positive"

My love for him didn't die

My life was full of different colors
You were the one who changed to it none
You made me see the reality I was not aware existed in love,
You showed me the worst in love
I still tried showing the best to you

The memories are still fresh
The bed sheet still has your fragrance
My heart still aches.
The hurt has made me hate love
But the love for you didn't die
Easier was to move on from you
Yet there remained a part that wanted the same you
Days were beautiful with you and with time it changed into something i never want, you made me realize how only love from one side wasn't enough to keep the sparkle between us alive.
That night was the last time I saw you, that night was the last time i was myself. With the broken pieces i walked away to never turn back
But little did i know your dreams will haunt like never before

But like all our happy memories the memory of that night is everything that still remains fresh, fresh enough to not go back to you.
We went apart but the love for him didn't die so fast.

Kya woh sachmein ishq tha

Bada ajeeb hain yeh ishq ka defination
Kabhi koi dosti kehta toh kabhi koi ussey andha
Maine inn sab ke beech khudne bhi ki dhundne ki iss jawab ko koshish
Jara aage hi badi thi khoj mein jab woh naujawan samne se aate dikha
Woh badi ajeeb sa ehsaas le aya tha dil mein mere
Sab haseen aur acha lagne ka jara asar shuru hua hi tha
Hasi sirf mere jubaan pe nai jara si uske mein bhi thi
Woh aakhon ke khel mein piche woh bhi nai
Kuch aage badhte hi ja rahe the inn khel mein akhon ke
Jab achanak woh pas aaye mere, baatein shuru ki puri raat tak jo chalti gayi humari
Raat khatam jab subha hui woh sapne ki tarah gayab tha bistar se mere
Yakeen tab hua unn dil jalein shayaro ki baaton par
Ki ishq humesha se dil se nai kai baar jism se hota hain
Woh jissey humne ishq socha tha woh subha apne raah jo chal baitha tha, pata tab laga dil ko ki jo pehli mulaqat bistar tak layein woh jane kaha sacha ishq hoga galti ki jo humne ussey ushq samaj kar jo ishq kabhi sacha na tha. "

Samriddhi Singh

Samriddhi Singh is a law student and simultaneously pursuing her management degree. She always aspired to be multi-talented and wanted to learn new skills and art other than academics. This lockdown has helped her explore the hidden writer within her. This poem is going to be the second published work. Apart from writing, she is a trained Bharatnatyam dancer and has a keen interest in painting and singing also.

For her, life is all about creating oneself. Recently, she started her YouTube channel
and still working on it to make it better. "

STOP FEMALE INFANTICIDE

Let me grow,
Don't cut me and throw,
I know I was difficult to sow,
But you put all your heart and soul,
Then why you don't want me to grow?
I won't let your head bow,
Will always go with the flow,
My branch will flourish only when you allow,
Will never dare to ask for more water to grow,
My fresh fruits will give your life a glow,
And I promise to always stay hallow,
But please let me grow."

Reshma kausar Mohideen

Reshma Kausar Mohideen (M.Com / B.ed) is a commerce professor. She loves to play with flavours in the kitchen and words in the books, she is an aspiring writer who is wishful to explore the amazing world of authors and strives really hard to amaze her readers with her stupendous write-ups.

Insta Handle: Sword_of_word_86"

INDIA OF MY DREAMS.

Long time ago, we called it 'A Golden Bird',
She is wounded now with her wings broken,
Her feathers have shed, she doesn't sing a word,
Flightless poor bird is no more golden.

I dream that INDIA paves her path in the light of its Constitution,
Religion becomes a less serious affair than employment, health & education.

A nation where democracy is practiced in true sense,
Where corruption is struck hard & citizens embrace non-violence.

India gets stained with the shades & tints of green.
The earth, water & air are non-toxic, hygienic & clean.

There is more food on a needy's plate than a dustbin,
Where a 'body alive' is valued more than the one in a coffin.

The farmers & workers are not compelled to commit suicide,
The core builders of the nation lead a healthy life with pride.

Where we all work as a team towards nation's development,
Where every citizen realise his accountability rather just blaming the government.

Women's modesty is heightened and men's gaze is lowered,
Where we respect emotions, 'naked' & prefer bodies, 'covered'.

We feel indisposed to shed blood and readily willing to donate,
Where the effects of technology is a topic of discussion, not debate.

I dream that her lost glory, she should regain,
and soar high in the global sky once again."

ELECTION OR ELOCUTION

It's time to beg for and steal the maximum votes,
To build a machine of printing dollars and notes.

It's time to hire some bribed domestic puppets,
And make them blow the tattered trumpets.

It's time to bury their artifice deep under the ground,
And to pop out like frogs in rain, and later, go unfound.

It's time to promise education, employment & health,
To cram the jars of their greed with the coins of luxuries and wealth.

It's time to spit lies after chewing the gum of truth,
To play with the trust of masses and fool the innocent youth.

It's time to visit the weeping lanes stinking with paucity,
To build their grand palaces on the founding stone of poverty.

It's time to act unbeatably to accomplish their illegitimate ambition,
To abuse the rival parties who are actually on the exact same mission.

It's time to make unrealistic and false promises,
To conquer hearts by shouting at the top of their voices.

It's time to wear the whitest of clothes to conceal their dark dreams,
To deliver the rote memorized speech without knowing what it means.

It's time to sink the boat of already drowning nation,
By giving the hopes of relief through the ropes of election.

Dr. Sarita Garg

शिक्षा: एम ए(अर्थशास्त्र एवं दर्शन शास्त्र, स्वर्ण पदक) डॉक्टरेट(दर्शन शास्त्र)
साहित्यिक: कविता लेखन, कहानी, आलेख लघु नाटिका लेखन रेडियो स्टेशन जोधपुर से विभिन्न प्रकार से जुड़ाव(आकस्मिक उदघोषक, नाट्य कलाकार, युववाणी कार्यक्रम संचालन) जोधपुर शहर के विभिन्न साहित्यिक संस्थाओं से जुड़ाव, वर्तमान में अनेक साहित्यिक ऑनलाइन संस्थाओं से जुड़ाव, कर्मस्थली भीलवाड़ा से साहित्य सृजन जारी।

कौन जाने वो कविता बन ही जाए

याद के जंगल को यूं न काट पागल
फिर नई फसलों की रुत आये न आये।
रुत, बहारें और नज़ारे आ भी जाएं
फिर यही मंज़र कभी आये न आये।
स्वप्न सारे क़ैद कर लो आँख में तुम
जाने कब ये झिलमिलाती रात आये।
रात तारों से भरी गर आ भी जाये
क्या खबर वो स्वप्न फिर न टिमटिमाएं।
वक़्त को क़दमों में मेहनत की गिरा दो
क्या मजाल उसकी कि वो न सर झुकाये।
हर हँसी के हर्फ़ को स्याही लगा दो
कौन जाने वो कविता बन ही जाए।।

स्मृतियों का इतिहास

दिन गुज़र जाते हैं, रातें भी गुज़र जाती हैं
याद वो शय है जो दिल में ठहर जाती है।
पल पल की सभी बातें रहती हैं दिल-औ-जान में
और देखते ही देखते स्वप्न भी महका जाती है।
क्या ज़रूरी है कि वक़्त ठहर जाए कहीं
यादें वक़्त की ज़ंजीर भी बन जाती है।
जब भी तन्हां या परेशान होता है मन
यादें अपनों की, पेशानी को सहलाती है।
सुनते आए हैं हम इतिहास के दोहराने की बात
देखें स्मृतियां कब अपना इतिहास दोहराती हैं।।

Jashu Sankhlecha

Jashu Sankhlecha this side, an adoring daughter of gautam Sankhlecha. She's a teenager of 18 ,persuing B.Com with Hairdressing and beauticianing. She is owner of @versatile_amateur on Instagram where she pens healing stories and lovely exotic fables which is loved by many listeners. She is engaged with her tagline of life; 'obsession and ambition'.

She gets inspiration from the great philosophers naming 'Gaur gopaldas' and 'Jay shetty' and from a well-known writer 'Ashish bagrecha'."

Hyy, me tanisha, 24 sal ki umra h meri, or aaj meri shaadi hai..
Uss shakhs se jisey me janti tak nahi hu
Or ham sirf ek baar milchuke hai shadi tey hone ke baad.
Sabki pehli mulaqaat kuch haseen si hoti hai.
Par meri..
Mere pass itne zakhmi shabhdh nhi hai baya karneko!
Ussdin hamne milkr sirf saudey kiye the..
Or soude me kuch esey bayaan bhi hai ki vo mujhse kbhi pyaar nhi karpaengey kyuki vo kiisi or se pyaar karte hai.
vo use kabhi bhula nahi payenge. Or yeah bhi bayaaa karke gae h vo ki yeah shadi vo unke parivar ke kehne par kar rahe hai!
Or vo mujhe pese ki koi kami aane nahi dengey!

Me tumse kuch puchna chahti hu,
-Kya poori zindagi sath bitane ke lie pesa kaafi hai?
-kya paisa mujhe har khushi desakta hai?
-kya paisa mujhe meri izzat Or mera haq desakta hai?

Mene bohot se sapne dekhey they meri shaadi ke lie.
Par ab na mere pass kuch pane ko hai ,na kuch khone ko!
Jo parivar paane jaari thi vo to pehle se hi paraya ho chuka hai..
Or ek parivar ko to me apne piche chorkar aa hi gai hu..
Me vo aayat banchuki hu jisey ab padhne me koi bhi shakhs dilchaspi nahi rakhta!

Me na writer hu na philosopher, par ek baat tumse kehna chahti hu..
Apni zindagi ke sare zaroori faisle jese ki shadi, career, sapne Or bhi bohot kuch! tum khud se lena, kisike behkaave me aakar nhi!!
Aise bohot se imtehaan ayengey tumhare samne, tumhara haqq hai apne raste khud chunna!!
Varna tum khud ki zindagi to tabah kar hi dogey Or shayad tumse jude logoki bhi..
Kher meri shaadi Or barbaad dono aaj hi ke din hai..
Congrats nhi kahoge?

Samruddhi Sharma

She is a kind of person who like to express her thoughts and emotions through writing.

(1)

Let you fear, feared from the fact that you don't fear about it at all. "

Adibah Masood

I'm Adibah Masood. I'm a designer student from Amity University. I love to write especially by getting inspired from real life conclusions. I want to be the person who can create a world with full of positivity and love.

I want to be the leader who motivates inspire and push others up.

I love to get engaged with peoples mind and their hearts and then i want someone to look at me and say because of you i didn't give up.

That's how i want to change the world, that's how i want to live."

CHILDHOOD MEMORIES

As we grow old childhood memories become the best part of our life. Undoubtedly, childhood memories can be termed as the heavens of a Man's life. Those were the life when we live life like kings. It's the part of human life with no stress, no worries or care in the world. Even if there were tensions we just don't care about them . The prime motive of life during childhood is fun and joy.

as we grow old we realize the most beautiful and valuable treasure is also in the childhood pictures which flashes one thousands memories of peoples, places, moments, feelings, laughter and smiles.

Those memories about childhood events and incidents shine like stars in the sky of our life looking at a photograph and wishing you could just re-live that moment over and over again.

It's true that childhood is like being drunk, everyone remembers what you did except you. There's something about those days, those times which you simply just can't replace.

I miss eating however much i wanted to without a thought,
I miss being carefree silly and messy without being judged,
I miss being not stressed.

Those were the days when feelings, people were not fake, when wounded knees were easy to heal than a broken heart , those were the days when friendship, promises everything was so pure and simple but what i miss the most of all, was the time which seemed to never run out .

Remember when we were kids and we wanted to grow up ? what exactly were we thinking ?

We didn't realize we were making memories we just knew we were having fun back then;

Those long summer vacations, visiting Naani's house, hopscotch, ice and water , hide and seek, pakdam-pakdai game, paper boat, scratched knees, messy hair and castle where dirt was the only makeup and a blushed look on that muddy face looked really good when mom had words to lecture upon.
Sometimes i wish to have a time machine so that i could just rewind back to the old days and press a pause just for a little while and want to feel few things again.
How can it be that my memories are more alive than i am?

Make sure that your life is full of happy memories.
Let's never stop making memories
Things end but memories last forever.
Sometime you have to accept the fact that certain things will never go back to the way they used to be.
Enjoy the little things in life, because one day you'll look back and will realize they were big and priceless things.
MEMORIES ARE GONE
But thank you for all the soft , sweet , carefree and valuable things you have left behind....in my home , in my head and in my heart....."

Srishti Srivastava

Raat ko andhera kahte hain
Srishti ko uss andhere ki roshni
Samandar jitna gahra hai
Uska dil uske apno ke liye utna bada hai
Actors jitne man se acting karte hain
Utne man se wo apni poems likhti hai
Jitni exciting se bachche sikhna chahte hain
utni exciting se usko padhne ki talab hai"

Dev Joshi

Baalveer ko janam diya
unko itna bada kiya
Dev unko naam diya
Hum sab ko ek idol diya
Uncle Aunty Aap dono
Hain kaise itne cute?
Dev bhaiya ko kaise
Lge honge aap rude?
Unko itna pyara or sweet bnaya
Sanskaar bhar bhar ke laya
Hum sab ko aap teeno
ka parivar itna bhaya
Hum sab ne aap teeno ko
Family and Idol bhi banaya
Maine dekha TV par
Pahli baar Baalveer jab
Aaya pasand bahot jyada
Jis din chhuta episode
us din mujhe rona aaya
Pata jab se chala mujhe
Dev Joshi unka naam hai
Uss din se aap log se milna
Ek hi Sapna Kaam hai
Poetry karne se mujhe
jo ek pahchan mili
main uski wjh se
aap logon se judi
Pasand aaun ya nahi
Main bas yahi
batana chahti hun
D3 Parivar ko
Kab se jaanti hun"

Dev Joshi ki Maa

Dev bhaiya ko aapne banaya
Baalveer unko naam dilaya
Cute si smile hmari aati
Aunty jab aap smile laatin
Aunty jab aap smile laati
Haay kya sharm aati
Maharaja mein baith kar
ek din aapke saath khana khaenge
Gujarat ke famous jagah par
aapke sath waqt bitaenge
kya aapko acha lgega
Apne ek member se milna
Apni beti aur uske
Apne Maa Papa ka aana
Ye poem kaisi lagi
Please aap mujhe btana"

Jennifer Rebecca Paul

Jennifer is a budding artist who writes poems, short stories, fictional and non-functional stories, she adores singing and is a very compassionate person do follow her on Instagram @025.lilian for more!

These days

Lifting myself up
Feels like a heavy burden inside me
And then, I think of my mother
That inexhaustible flame
That kept her alive
Until she was gone.

She knew all about love and life
And how pain felt
She knew how to make her child happy
She knew how cruel and beautiful life was
She was a friend indeed
Just like the fire burning in the cold winter,
Her presence is unforgettable."

Darshitha P Mandoth

Darshitha P Mandoth is born and brought up in Bangalore, Karnataka, India, a student studying law in Christ University who is an optimistic enthusiast, ambitious, talented, crazy about bikes and enjoys racing. She dislikes negative attitude and lies. Writing these magnificent poems makes her feel lively midst everyday's monotonous routine and believes that

only the person knows oneself the best. Writing poems is what drives her but not to forget the only goal for her life is serving her country! We look forward to reading her many more beautiful poems.

I'll Be There

When you swade away from the noise,
When you elope yourself to a quiet place...
Still you can hear some mutters out of the noise!
The cold breeze on your dripping sweat,
Those dim lights of the city midst the tall trees;
A place far away on the heights;
Where your mind feels lively,
Thou your thoughts as fresh as the breeze of sunrise.
When all you can hear is the chirpping birds,
With a vision that shades all the sadness apart!
Let's bring back those days,
That's utterly vanished midst the proud crowd;
The irritable laughter of the games,
I might have not been there for you yesterday,
I'm sorry I changed but trust me;
After this... I'm here,
I'm here not for now but forever;
Because the true joys lay in the happiness
of the ones you care about,
of the ones you love,
of the ones who are there for you no matter what!
25th May 2020

Sakshi Jain

Co-author Sakshi Jain is a good writer from Hathras
She has completed her diploma and currently pursuing B.tech
She has been writing poetry from 1 year as her passion.
She wants to be a self-publishing author in future.

Follow her writings on instagram: @_shenu_writings_"

(1)

तलाश है उसकी जो मुझे कभी मिला ही नही
तलाश है उसकी जो पता नही है भी या नही
तलाश है उसकी जो मुझे संभालेगा और समझेगा
तलाश है उसकी जो सीने से लगाकर मेरे दर्द सुनेगा
तलाश है उसकी जो मेरे आँसू पोछेगा
तलाश है उसकी जो पता नही कभी मिलेगा भी या नही
यूँ तो सब साथ है पर इस दिल को आज भी बस उसी की तलाश है।।"

Aahan Agarwal

A student of class 11 from Bhilwara, Rajasthan he loves to write and talk about Life.

A Landscape

The night was too mesmerized,
With the well-lit moon,
The twinkling stars,
And the colour it wears-
Black,
It was a landscape where,
The tears were hidden,
Like the sun behind the mountains,
In a child's landscape,
And as the night got deeper,
The tears came out,
As the sun shines,
With the deepening of day,
Who knows the day and night?
The sun and tears,
The mountains and the moon,
The stars and,
The stars and the smile,
All were within two piece of,
Papers-
Beautifully drawn by an-
Innocent child,
Who doesn't know
What his lines say,
What the lines in his drawing-
Hide,
And why is the landscape,
His favourite drawing-
Ever?
Forever?

Janani

Janani is a budding artist who writes poems, short stories, quotes and many more, she dances her heart out and pens down her emotions into books and papers, her love for nature and wildlife is unceasing.

In the end, we are all masked up

You wore the mask of happiness during your pain
You wore the mask of willingness though you were hesitant
You wore the mask of strength during your vulnerability
You wore the mask of courage during your times of fears
You wore the mask of hope during your time of dismay
You wore the mask of silence when the demons inside of you craved to scream
You wore a mask portraying somebody else while you wanted to be yourself
In the end, we are all masked up."

Dhanya Ravi

Dhanya Ravi, a life science graduate from Coimbatore, Tamil Nadu is currently a freelancer. She is a very expressive and enthusiastic person. First, she started to pen her thoughts into simple poems and quotes. She then wanted to spread positivism in all possible ways, so she started her YouTube channel ""dhanii thoughts"" where she tells moral and motivational stories. Her long-time goal to own a blog was recently accomplished with support from her husband. In her blog ""dhaniithoughts"" - thoughts of a girl she covers simple life topics we all come across, with only positivism as the essence. Other than writing she is also fond of dance. Her love to connect with people through writing has made her a part of this anthology.

My Wings to fly

I am the princess with invisible crown
No one can ever let me down

Born as little angel with wings to fly
Then why so shy, let me try
And fly so high to reach the sky
To see the spark in my own eye

I want to be so much bold
Even when I become very old
My mind is very clear like a moon
That to born as a girl is a boon

My voice is not so soft and so loud
But I love myself and I am so proud

When I am angry, I might scream
But I always focus to reach my dream
My thoughts may not be always logic
Also, I believe in some great magic

Because I have the magic wand
Made full of power in my hand
I don't want to live like a fish in a pool
When I can rock the world and be so cool

Women are born as human on earth
With a heart full of warmth
She can get all the evil things fired
And do something good, to make others get inspired

Let me shine like a star very bright

And live my life happily, this is my right...

So, let me fly ...high...so high...
With my wings to reach the sky …

Broken

Breaking down inside into pieces
But I see smiles at those faces
Which never showed me any traces
That made me realise the invisible laces
That struck around my neck and hurts at places ...
I started to hear some sweet voices
Still it took some time to know I made wrong choices...
Later, I found that the lace's one end lies in hands of that fake smiling faces
And shocked to see the other end in the hands of those sweet voices ...
Don't believe anyone except yourself
At times ... test yourself to make sure, you are being your own self ....and not changed by any chance or choice ...

Akanksha Gupta

Akanksha from Jamshedpur Jharkhand, is an animal lover, volatile bilingual professional writer , a solivagant , wanderer searching for anecdote in the glittering eyes of various elements of society.

With an enigmatic mind, social issues tends her to spill ink seamlessly on the paper as she is an empathizer and want to be the change herself via her writings and actions before asking for change. She is bearer of fire for change produced by her nib cutting across the paper.

Not a license to rape

Born in stereotype,
With only that sort of prototype
Her aspirations were
Simply food for his desperation.

Patriarchal dominance,
Her sub ordinance,
A sense of hovering fear,
With a thought - ""ohh all over again!""

Whirling views of downward spiral,
She was on viral,
But, but he was ready to embark,
On ugly grips and fretting soul marks.

Her body needed some rest,
But he leaped on her breasts,
Caring about her least
Pondering into her tired body

Those cruel marks of undressing,
Wildly his nails scratching,
Painfully injecting his dagger,
Quenching his thirst, till he makes her burst.

The four walls all mocking at her,
It was a wed lock,
Which wasn't easy to unlock
Screams and yell in pain all gone in vain.

Bulging eyes, mascara soiled,
It was now for almost every night,
She had to go through this fright,
And her only cure was in the form of passive endure.

But the point is up to when?
Upto when, one marriage is licence to rape,
And when will one get the escape
For now it's time to support the cause.

Speak up against Marital Rape
Go for healthy and happier intimate shape
Forceful intent will no longer be the say,
Will and consent is the only way.

Ishaa Suresh

Ishaa Suresh, a writer who likes to experiment with her pieces in all the genres where she pens down her opinions and justifications about the things she notices in herself as well as the society. She gets quite content and light-hearted after working on a pen script and she looks forward to writing more of these throughout in the future.

ROUTINE RULE

I'm thinking maybe a considerable
Amount of decades ago, a family
Somewhere in the north of India
The bride would have decorated herself
With mehendi on her hands and a child
Must have wanted the same and maybe
Everyone did so too. A few families must
Have adapted it and now we call it a ritual.

Somewhere around the country,
A woman who just lost her husband
Must have been in shock and her
Relatives would have helped her
With cooking or she must have been
Emotionally weak to come outside for
A few days and again, goes the adaption
And now we call it a must, I'm guessing.

Habits root from the background of
Comfort or the situations at hand,
We continue to do the same maybe
Because it makes us happy or maybe
We think that's the only right way to be.
Who defines the right? And if so, what
Really is wrong. In fact, actions that do
Come from doing something different
Is what makes them regular or routine.

Swati Nayak

Swati Nayak is currently pursing Bachelors from Miranda House,University of Delhi. She derives her writing inspiration from nature and wildlife. She uses poetry as a means to pour out her emotions on paper, to make people smile or relate to.

Growth

Beneath the tree canopy,
Bright specks of sunshine,
Prance with the breeze on the ground.
The foliage starts serenading
sweetly as a whisper.
Shrivelled leaves and twigs,
precipitate softly on wet earth.
There's loss but no regrets,
The tree grows on !

It extends its massive boughs,
Aiming at the sun.
Delicate young leaves and inflorescence adorn
Its vast green plumage.
The nature welcomes them with kisses of
Cool, wet dewdrops.
Amidst all this joy,
The tree grows on.

Diksha Motwani

Diksha Motwani is a passionate girl from Mumbai, Maharashtra. She loves to pen her feelings. She is introvert but her pen makes her extrovert. She is a writer, singer, artist and a poet!

Can I?

I really dont know,
What this wierd feeling is for,
I just wanna hug you tight,
And cry out all whats inside,
Just wanna have your shoulder,
To make me relief,
I just really dont know why am feeling lone and low,
Can you please be here for me?
Can I please cry?
Can I hug you?

Ganesh Sadashiv Patil

This Is Ganesh Sadashiv Patil.He Is The Student Of UG In Field Of Pharmacy. He Has Writer And Poet Who Writes 50+ Poetry In Hindi And Marathi Languages. He Loves To Write On Love, Humanity, Motivation And Social Themes. He loves to write down his feelings, his thoughts on various topics which make him a writer of one his own kind.

प्यार की रात

ए रात मेरे दिल में तू आ याद मुझको उसकी तू देती जा
मिले थे हम जीस दिन उस दिन की याद मुझे तू देती जा
प्यार किया था जीससे मैने उसकी खुशबू तू फैहलाती जा
उसकी चेहरे की रौनको को तू मेरे इन नैनो में यु बसाती जा
राह पर जीस चल पडे थे हम उस राह को तु भी बताती जा
मंजिल जो तय की थी साथ हमने उस जीतकी खुशी देती जा
वो थी खयालो में बसी मेरे उन खयालो को ताजा करती जा
सपने जो मैने देखे थे उसके उन सपनो की बाते तू करती जा
हसी उसकी जो होती थी चेहरे पर ऐसी हसी तू दिखाती जा
रूपको उसके जो निहारता हूं उस रूप को दिल में बसाती जा
प्यार मेरा इस दिल में तुम्हारा जो बरसो से यहा है बसा हुआ
इस प्यार के इन लम्हो को हरवक्त दिल में मेरे तू बसातीही जा

Kareena Verma

she is a computer science student and co-author of many anthologies and just like her name Kareena delineate alike her name , sanguine with her soul, pure with her heart , innocent with her straightforward thoughtful perceptions!
For her Rectitude within her is everything & nothing is above than Veracity with our nation , she wants only to flame alike terracotta Diya, for one day she'll spread the happiness of lights as the most bright star in the sky of someone home and wanna to spread love of humanity everywhere! "

Teenage Aroma

The memories....
This is the age of full on fun & joy &
Pressurised life with burden of beg full on with books
Started with nursery class, yeah with alphabet translation
""A for apple""
""B for ball"" and ""C for cat"" and......
Here we go , with ""D for Dead""
Fallowing & chasing the rate life race
In the tough competition of getting the first Position in the class, otherwise you fell asleep with less marks & grades,
Growing age with knowledge of bundles & fall in silly feeling with "" L for Love"" and then you will killing your time
In break-up and catch-up !
And then our school life will finished with lots of Blessings and memorable memories that's never come back again!

vitriolage

I still take a trip down memory lane,
Those horrible moments seriously so insane,

How I suffer the loss of wisdom of my Stunner,
Stitching the my burnt face, body & eyelids,

After ten hours felt asleep with burnt face
I closed myself in those black shadow cage

Dreadfully burnt me with sulphuric acid,
Torment a long, ache & scars
Melting alike polythene in my body of flaccid,

Mental tortured , fearful nightmares
And crying terrifying screams
I hate myself when I see mirror front of me

But you threw acid on my face ,
Not on my dreams & self-esteem! "

Bhuvan

His name is Bhuvan & he is 19 Years Old. Living in Sirsa, Haryana.

Studying in B.Tech Civil Engineering at JCDM College Of Engineering, Sirsa

He is not so good at poetries but still learning & doing efforts to be good. His Instagram Account Is @noob.poet."

इस दिल में प्यार भरा है सिर्फ तुम्हारे लिए।

दिल में भरकर प्यार अपना
हम चल दिये हैं लुटाने को,
दिख जाऊं तुम्हे, मैं राहों में कहीं
बुला लेना मुझे हँसाने को,

इस प्यार पर हक़ तुम्हारा भी है
जितना चाहे ले लेना, और याद रखना इस दीवाने को,
ज़िन्दगी में कभी भी दिल करे तो बुला लेना
ये मसख़रा आ जायेगा तुम्हे हँसाने को,

रोना मत जीवन में कभी तुम
हम दूर कर देंगे तुम्हारे सभी दुखों को,
परेशानियों की राह मोड़ देंगे तुम्हारे ख़ातिर
बस तुम अपना मान लेना इस दीवाने को,

दिल में भरकर प्यार अपना
हम चल दिये हैं लुटाने को,
दिख जाऊं तुम्हे, मैं राहों में कहीं
बुला लेना मुझे हँसाने को।

चलते ख़त।

जीवन की तमाम उलझनों में फँसा था
सहसा सुन पड़ा कि, मेरे नाम का एक ख़त आया है,

ना जाने किसने भेजा और क्यों
मेरा दिल अभी तक यह जान न पाया था,

शाम को अपने कमरे पर पहुँचा जब मैं
उस ख़त पर नाम मेरी माँ का देख ये दिल बहुत मुस्काया है,

कुछ लोग सोचते हैं,
भला एक माँ के ख़त में ऐसा क्या जादू है?

और मैं इस राज़ को जान गया हूँ कि,
माँ तो खुद में ही एक जादूगर है।

Krishna Motwani

Krishna Motwani is a Student currently.
She use to pen down her feelings.
She is a moody girl.
She started writing in the month of june,2020.
She writes in her free time.
She writes some motivational quotes or poetries too and practices artworks also.
She lives her life like a bird
As bird flies freely and enjoys life like that she also lives her life freely and enjoy fullest.

Be bold!

Dark phases comes to start a new journey with smile on face,
We have solution but we can't find at the moment to fight with problems.

We have to stay strong,
We shouldn't care if we are not wrong.

We don't have to go back,
Just have to fight and awake.

We all know, through these dark phases we get stressed,
Yes! I know our life is fully messed.

Yes! I know it's hard to fight,
But at the end we just feel to hug life tight.

Hardships are part of our journey always,
They will be there to make to strong and find your best ways."

Adira Singh

She is a school going student and has taken part in many anthologies and has also won many prizes for the same. She is also a keen horse rider and is a state level swimmer.

Shades of Ink

Ink flows through my hands
Only to blot couple of pages
Some letters and some spaces

My pages are blank, and words are things
But a drop of ink, upon a thought
Produces, perhaps makes millions think

Anger spilling Red and love blushing Pink
Smudging lines on white paper like night, Black ink
Moody blues and mysterious hues

It is that flaming ink, that inspire my thoughts
Line by line and moment by moment
made quiet and still feelings heard dipped in ink

Seldom does a pen write more fluidly
than one held with heartache and pain
To readers it is just some words; to us it is all our world.

Reema

Reema! A 20 year old budding poetess, who writes anything what goes on in her mind or is felt by heart. Shaping the thoughts in lyrical and aesthetic way is what she loves the most. Her writing is inspired from what she feel, understand and learn from life as well as from the people around her. She believe that stories can take one to a beautiful world of imagination where every emotion is clearly felt and understood."

A Letter To My Ex

Hey !
Kya tu sun rahi hain kya mujhe ?
I know, bahot din huye hain hume baat kiye huye,
I know, pehle jaisa kuch nhi rha hain,
I know, ki pehle jaisa kuch hoga bhi nhi,
But,
Aaj bhi tumhara wait kr raha hu ki tu call nhi toh text kregi ,aur puchegi how're you?
Aaj bhi tumhe bahot yaad krta hu,
Haan! Par tumhe nhi hamari un yaadonko jo ki aaj sirf yaadein hain
I don't know whether to cry or smile,whenever i remember those days.
Par aaj bhi hamare photos dekhta hu na toh
Somehow,i feel numb deep inside.
aaisa lagta hain ki tu phir mere paas aaye.
Tum loutke aana kabhi toh un yaadonke shehar mein sirf tehlne ke liye...mere dil mein basera bankar rehne ke liye nhi!
Tumhare sath beete huye din kuch aalag se hi feelings and experiences diya krte the
We were imperfectly perfect together!
Par mujhe aaj tak samajh nhi aaya ki why you left ?
Aaj bhi tumhe bhulne ki koshish krta hu,
Aaj bhi tumhare bare mein naa likhne ki koshish krta hu,
Aaj bhi tumse hate krne ki koshish krta hu,
Par mujhe ye sab krne se rokna chahiye,
Haan ! Mein yeh letter tumhe dena chahta hu
But i can't.
Remember...Tum mera aakhri ishq ho
Because ,for a one ,for a change
I believe that aakhri ishq lasts forever and ever and ever!!!
Isilye mein isey post kr raha hu ki mere jaise kisi ko toh iski help ho jaye.
Take care. Bye !

Meharun Halidha

Meharun Halidha, hails from Tirunelveli, Tamilnadu. She completed her schooling from Rose Mary Model School and is pursuing Industrial Biotechnology in GCT, Coimbatore. She is a good orator and writer. She wrote 20+ anthologies and still counting. A passionate engineer to pen her thoughts.

Laughter

Laughter is the foundation of reconciliation. — St. Francis de Sales

Have you ever smiled at strangers in your first meet? People say 'First impression is the best impression'. If this is true, then your smile makes a greater part.

"Smiles are soul's kisses"

Have your ever thought to lead a stress-free life? Then you must definitely laugh often. Laughter strengthens your immune system, boosts mood, diminishes pain so that you could lead a stress-free life.

"Against the assault of laughter, nothing can stand. Even Stress can't!"

Have you ever felt being lonely? The first which you have to do is 'Laugh'. Laughter creates social bonds, reduces pain and anxiety. The more you laugh , more occupied you are.

"Laughter is the shortest distance between two people."

Personally, I am a cool and optimistic person. People used to ask me about my coolest nature. The secret of my energy is nothing but my "Smile". I am a girl who smiles a lot even at bad times. My Smile give me strength and even hope. My Smile is my friend who will never leave me at any cost. And I always make others smile which is the most essential one. Making fun of self is a greatest Humour.

"Laugh at yourself first, before anyone else can."

Humour is a greatest gift of god. It is one good thing which could be shared with others every time.

“ Humour is mankind’s greatest blessing”

Laughter is a greatest medicine. Feel free to laugh every time. Having a smily face doesn’t mean that you are easily cheatable. It only means you are a positive vibe. You can improve your emotional health, strengthen your relationships, find greater happiness and even add years to your life. People with stronger sense of humor were found to live longer in spite of illness, especially cardiovascular disease and infection. They say “Funny or die”.

“He who laughs, lasts!”

Let us not use bombs and guns to fight. Use this greatest weapon. “Laughter”. There or here, moon or sun, black or white, Good or bad, whatever it is. I laugh. I always! Remember this! A very little is needed to make happy life.

As soap is to body, laughter is to soul!!!!!"

Jayashree Sahoo

Jayashree Sahoo is habitant of ODISHA .
Her writings started on yourquote, notojo and mirakee like writing platforms. You can search her on yourquote by name of Jaya Jayashree . Nowadays She is member of many writing communities and earned a alots of certificates through her writings .
She is Co.author of 200+ anthologies .Also She is Compiler of many anthologies in Hindi ,English and Odia languages . Currently She is working as project head and board member of a reputed publication .
Also she has interested in singing ,travelling,photography also. Among of these extra activities She studying Nursing on govt medical and she has an aim for be a RN nurse and good writer .

One promise for you

Hey my beloved ,
Do u want to listen my midnight melodies ,
In which the song's lyrics are dedicating to you only ,
There so many loves from my inner heart in that melodies ,
Do you want to sleep in my lap once in this midnight ,
If you sleep ,'m sure will be blush ,
Still , will concentrate into your eyes ,
And 'll drench in your deep love ,
Yes ,Darling
So many thoughts are in mind to take you ,
But there ,ll search for a little chance to clear all this ,
When you added with my life..
My wish, my desire
My night, my day
All are favour of you
Promised you, today..
May be foots won't with ur foot always..
Still, the end of my last breath
I""ll try to be stay with you..
Like ur shadow of ur body
I for you
You for me
Give you my words..
Spend my tym
Every day and night
Always with you
Give you my promise
Bring shiny star
If you once beg
Always for you..

Shivani M.R.Joshi

Co-author Shivani is a good writer from Ahmedabad , Gujarat. She is only 20 years old.

She has completed her Education in science stream. She has been writing poetry for last six months as her passion. For the past some days, she has been published among the people in the form of a writer, she write many encouraging stories and many poems and some of her writings has been printed in many books. She wants to be a doctor in future."

Akelepn se 1 bat sikhi he,
Bhot sukun deta he akelepn,
Beshak chahere pr muskuraht
nhi lata,
Pr ykin mano kbhi ankho me
ansu bhi nhi ane deta. "

S. Vasha Varthini

Creative person with optimistic vibes. Working as assistant professor in the department of English. Love to learn new things always. Flow of emotions and thought penned through the form of writing. Explore the world through the penning.

Ink

Flow of blood struck the heart door
Flow of ink flows out in the nib tip
Shed of blood from heart was unrevealed
Dots of ink as words revealed to every eyes
Loud shouts in the streets useless
Silent scratch of ink penned powered
Shades of tears marked
In drops of ink spread over
Curve of lips
Dressed with beauty of ink
Shattered of splashes
Dipped of tiny dots covered as ink
Rhythmic sound unheard in those ink
Its penned as unheard melodies of heart
World without a poem
Soul without breath. . "

Abhishek Ghosh

Born in Kolkata, West Bengal, India. Grew up in Kolkata and Siliguri. A PGDM Graduate and a working professional in the Banking and Finance Sector.
Author of the Following Books:
1. Every Frame is a Painting (Novel Nuggets Publisher)
2. Love, Realization and The World of Today - A collection of Poems. (Juggernaut Books)
3. The Paradise Conflict (Novel Nuggets Publisher)

Interests in life:
READING | PHOTOGRAPHY | TRAVELLING | BLOGGING"

Scared

Scared, as I am of the world!
Not with the pandemic!
But, with people,
The violent nature of some people!
Scared, as I am of the world!

Scared, as I am of the world,
For the people,
I care,
For the people,
I love,
For the people,
I am close with!

Scared, as I am of the world,
Scared of those who hide their intention,
Like the criminals!

Scared, I am of the world,
These so-called civilized criminals,
May hurt the people,
I love and care!
Scared, I am in this world!

Scared, I am in this world!
We, humans, failed!
We, humans, failed to educate!
Scared, I am in this world,

Scared, I am in this world!
For the people, I love,
For the people, I care!

Where the system fails to protect the victim,
The criminals are out on a bail to commit crimes,
Scared, I am in this world,
Scared, I am in this world!

My lord, deliver us the justice,
Justice for the innocent lives,
And the criminals suffer,
So, that I can break bones and teeth of the vicious criminals!

Lord, give me the strength to stand for those who are innocent,
Irrespective of what they are and their choices,
Lord, give me the strength to fight for the people,
To fight for the innocent,
Lord, the innocent must not suffer,
Whoever they are,
Whatever their personal choices are,
There is no right for anyone to commit a crime!

Lord, give me the strength,
Not to be Scared, I am in this world,
Not to be Scared, I am in this world!
Not to be Scared, I will fight for the world,
Not to be Scared, I will fight for the innocent!

I am just no-one,
I do not want to be identified of whatever I am,
Just a heart to fight for the world!
Not to be Scared, I will fight for the world,
Not to be Scared, I will fight for the innocent!

Seemabharti

Seemabharti is a school student. She is very passionate about the writing. She inspired by William Shakespeare autobiography. She wants to be a great writer. She is only18 years old.

हम सफर बना लो""

मुझे अपने हर दर्द का हमदर्द बना लो
दिल में नहीं तो ख्यालों में बैठा लो
सपनों में नहीं तो आंखों में सजा लो
अपना एक सच्चा अहसास बना लो।।

मुझे कुछ इस तरह से अपना लो
अपने दिल की धड़कन बना लो
मुझे छुपा लो सारी दुनिया से
कि अपना एक गहरा राज़ बना लो।।

करो मुझ से मोहब्बत इतनी कि
अपनी हर एक चाहत का अंजाम बना लो
ढक लो मुझे अपनी जुल्फों में
कि मुझे अपना संसार बना लो।।

आप फ़ूल बन जाओ मुझे भंवरा बना लो
आप चांदनी बन जाओ मुझे चांद बना लो
रख दो अपना हाथ मेरे हाथों में
इस तरह कि मुझे अपने जीवन का हमसफर बना लो।।"

Srijanie

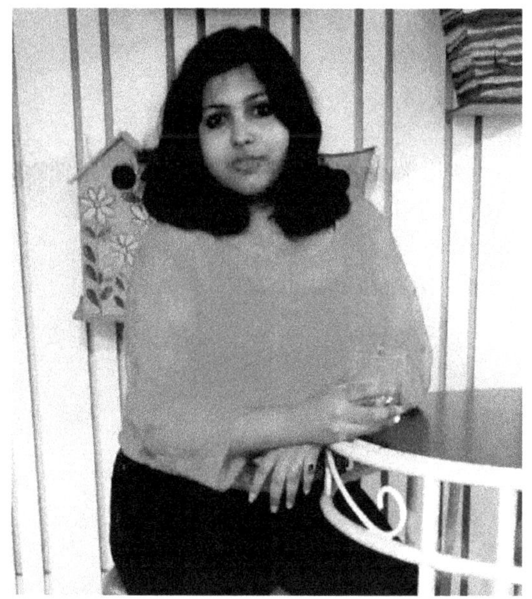

Born and raised in the City Of Joy, Srijanie Banerjee writes picturesque. She always urged to write since childhood and draws inspiration from the reality and inspirations of life. Her compositions speaks of love and witfulness inspired from lively drift.

The darkness of aeon

In the splendour of time,
Engulfs the antagonism and liberates all.
The enamoured of intimacy 'tween us
Fades in the distinct terrain of fear twirl.
And after that disconnection.

A life of space and integrity,
Self-esteem and identity-
One is not alone;
The soul is one's honest comrade.

Cage the Carcass

The exploitation can cage the body
But the soul is unbind.

The scratches of those abuses
The claw that forces pillage;
The scrape for pleasure,
Or maybe for seizure
The bust of fervours to bend the bod;
The creep in the head,
Or the frenzy rot
The phallus urge to curb the right-

The maraud confiscates the physical carcass
But cannot incarcerate the soul.

For between the limb it's just your spice
Shows how much you can be a vice.
The tomb will make her rest-
And free her soul from all your zest.

Sujish Kandampully

Being a graduate in Electrical Engineering and a passionate Writer, Sujish is also an Entrepreneur, Nutritionist, Blogger, Author, Photographer & a Philanthropist. He is recognized as an International Poet on Poetry Soup which is world's largest community of international poets.

He is also the author of the book ""Soul Strings"" published by YourQuote. Most of his works are based on his personal life experiences. You can find his work on platforms like YourQuote and Writco.

I Come From The Future

As time passed by
I kept learning life's toughest lessons,
And, it kept healing me from inside.

Today, I stand strong
Learning from my past experiences
That life is never easy as it seems to be
And it will never be

Accept this truth and move ahead in life
God has thrown us into the war zone
And we are fighting daily to survive.

Remember, this is just the beginning
Because the worst is yet to come...
This is my message to you
As I come from the future!"

Roar of the Lion

They said I'm weak
I cannot confront the people I meet
They called me stupid and nerd
Whenever I raised my voice no one heard
Blamed me for mistakes I never committed
No one to help around I felt broken and frustrated
But,
It's time to be strong now
Because if you stay silent today
It will be too late for you to even speak
It's time to raise the voice now
It's time for the lion to roar now."

Karan Singh

Student
Writing is my passion
I write what i feel"

Alvida

Keh do na,
Alvida buri yaadon se.
Keh do na,
Un zakhamon se..
Keh do na,
Zara alvida..
Keh do na.
Alvida

Duniya

Ye duniya,
Zaalim nhi hai..
Isme rehne wale log zaalim hai..
Unke irade,
Bekar hai..
Farak nhi hai,
Janwar or insaan mein..
Unki soch,
Bekr hai..
Zaalim hai unki soch,
Zaalim hai unke irade
Duniya nhi,
Log zaalim hai"

Kaushiki Sarkar

Bonjour bibliophile! Welcome to the journey of scribbling of Kaushiki Sarkar, a fellow writer and painter. Since 11th May, 2004 she is an earthling. Her journey of writing started in the beginning of year 2020. Her genre of writing is mainly based on motivation, inspiration, love, life, short stories, philosophy and other social problems.

LOVE

You are my love poetry.
Your love are the words
That ink my void heart."

Let your soul to tangle with mine

Let your arms be free
To hold and embrace me.
Let your soul to tangle with mine
As you kiss my tears of agony
And caress my scars.
Let me curl up in your arms,
With your fingers intertwined
And feel your soulful heartbeat
Before life in me fades.

Flairs and Glairs, a platform by a student for the students. We are esteemed youth struggling to carve out our path for our future and we follow a basic mindset Since everyone is not born with all-round skills. Joining hands with people who are born to execute it with perfection is the best way to evolve. Self-Evolution is the need of the hour but, evolving as a community is what we strive for. The initiative as kickstarted by, Founder- Mr. Shubham Shah with the motive to utilize the skillset and talent of writing has now a team of 10+ people who are actively participating into newer forms of learning and discovering talents among youngsters. We Provide platform and services like Publishing opportunities, Open mics, Workshops, Hands-on training. Operating with Brand Name of Flairs and Glairs (Publication House), we offer the chance of elevating a passionate writer to an esteemed author With Brand name Teekhe Zasbaaat. We bring to you an opportunity to get accustomed with the Public Speaking and Presenting of Thoughts along with regular challenges to brush up your inking spirit. The newest initiative to extend our services we introduced in a new writing Platform- The Glittering Fables and Ink Over Tears.

We Choose to Fly Like A Falcon than to be

a Leg Pulling Crab.

www.ingramcontent.com/pod-product-compliance
Ingram Content Group UK Ltd.
Pitfield, Milton Keynes, MK11 3LW, UK
UKHW022004190726
13853UKWH00004B/1724

9 789390 416882